PUGGLETON PARK

PENELOPE AND THE CURSE OF THE CANIS DIAMOND

For Abby, Monty, and Willa—DK

To Georgina—HP

PENGUIN WORKSHOP
An imprint of Penguin Random House LLC, New York

First published in the United States of America by Penguin Workshop,
an imprint of Penguin Random House LLC, New York, 2024

Text copyright © 2024 by Deanna Kizis
Illustrations copyright © 2024 by Penguin Random House LLC

Visit us online at penguinrandomhouse.com.

Library of Congress Cataloging-in-Publication Data is available.

Printed in the United States of America

ISBN 9780593661277 (paperback)
ISBN 9780593661284 (library binding)

1st Printing

LSCC

Design by Jay Emmanuel

PUGGLETON PARK

PENELOPE AND THE CURSE OF THE CANIS DIAMOND

by Deanna Kizis
illustrated by Hannah Peck

Penguin Workshop

CHAPTER ONE

Penelope the pug—clever, resilient, and happy, with a wonderful home and a kind heart—never wanted to go on an adventure again.

I'm not one of those pugs who takes risks purely for pleasure, she thought as she awoke one fine morning, *for I believe pleasure can just as easily be found in a soft bed next to a warm fire.*

Ever so contented, she stretched and

yawned until her belly popped out and her pink tongue curled. She did not have anything to do that day except to eat, play with Lady Diggleton, and nap, which meant it was to be a glorious day indeed.

Wait a moment, she thought, sitting up. *I do believe I had a most frightening dream.* She tried to remember before the memory flew away like a butterfly, as dreams often do. Oh, yes! She'd dreamed that she was lost again in Puggleton Park, and it was all the fault of a most dreadful squirrel.

If you have not met Dreadful Squirrel, then you should know that he has shifty eyes, buckteeth, and a sparse tail, and that he is more vexing than any other squirrel alive.

In the dream, Penelope was chasing Dreadful Squirrel, but he got away, as he always did, and Penelope realized she was very lost indeed. Without her owner, the only friend she had was Moon, whom you must know as well, since Moon shines in the sky for us all. It wasn't until Penelope met Lady Diggleton that her luck began to change. But that is another story altogether.

In *this* story, Penelope was relieved to realize that her dream was just that. She still lived with her dear Lady Diggleton in a brick house in Mayfair, London. Abby was still the lady's maid, Miss Bakerbeans was still the cook (and made the most delicious dog biscuits), and Lady Picklebottom,

Lady Diggleton's dearest friend, found dogs a bit more tolerable than she once did.

On her way downstairs, Penelope passed Abby, who was carrying a basket of laundry that smelled of lavender and soap. Abby smiled.

"Good morning, Penelope.

I hope you're having a fine day,"
she said. "I'd stop to pet you, but I
simply have too much work to do!"

Abby was always bustling about, so
Penelope made her way down another
flight of stairs to reach the first floor,
where she let herself out of her own
doggy door. This rather clever addition
was recently installed by a talented
carpenter, and it allowed Penelope to
go do her business in a most private
manner. (And she often had quite a
lot of business to do!)

Once she was finished, Penelope
entered the large pale green dining
room where the sunlight streamed
through the crystals in the chandelier
and made rainbows dance on the walls.
This was her favorite room in the

house, for it is where she often found her dear Lady Diggleton.

"Good morning, Penelope," Lady Diggleton said with a smile. She was seated at the enormous dining room table, eating her breakfast.

In response, Penelope wagged her tail and let out a small yelp, which meant, "And a very good morning to you."

She allowed Lady Diggleton to give her a scratch behind her left ear— this was her favorite spot, after all— then attacked the food in her silver dog bowl and licked it clean until it shone like new.

"It is time to go out, Penelope," Lady Diggleton said, standing and heading into the hall as the little pug followed.

"We are due at the offices of the *Morning Post*, where we shall buy an advertisement for the Ladies' Society for the Relief of Lost Dogs. Then I shall take you for a walk through Puggleton Park, and after that we shall return home in time for tea."

Penelope waited patiently as Lady Diggleton attached her leash, which was made of pale green leather to match her Lady's coat. She had not been expecting such a busy day, to be sure, but she did not find it disagreeable—as long as she was not going on an adventure, you see, for Penelope was quite through with those.

CHAPTER TWO

The offices of the *Morning Post* in Covent Garden were filled with people hurrying about in a self-important way. Penelope tried not to get trampled by the boots of reporters while Lady Diggleton met with Mr. Tippletattle, an editor who sounded most competent indeed.

"And what would you like your advertisement to say, Lady Diggleton?"

he asked, his pencil perched between his teeth just so.

"I should like it to say, 'Lady Diggleton and Lady Picklebottom are honored to announce that they shall be holding a ladies' sale of delightful, interesting, and rare things such as bangles, ribbons, and tea cozies,'" she said. "'The sale will benefit their charity, the Ladies' Society for the Relief of Lost Dogs,

which places unhoused dogs with families of good character.' "

Few were surprised to hear that Lady Diggleton had started a charity for lost dogs—she had rescued Penelope, after all. But the fact that her friend Lady Picklebottom was participating came as more of a shock. Lady Picklebottom used to say quite frequently that she believed all dogs belonged on a farm.

However, she had grown rather fond of Penelope—even going so far as to give her a new toy. This did not mean, however, that Lady Picklebottom had a dog of her own. *"That,"* she said when asked, "would be going one paw too far."

"I daresay, Lady Diggleton, I've heard that your society has become quite popular," Mr. Tippletattle said. He leaned forward and lowered his voice. "One of our reporters heard that your charity has caught the attention of the Queen, if you know what I'm saying."

Lady Diggleton gasped. "Whatever do you mean?"

"Mark my words," he said. "You are very much on Her Majesty's mind."

Eyes wide, Lady Diggleton paid for

her advertisement, while Penelope
wondered why Mr. Tippletattle couldn't
just tell Lady Diggleton everything
he knew. *This is the difference between
people and pugs,* she thought. *People
often prefer not to say what they are
thinking, while pugs prefer to say exactly
what they think—and mean it, too.*

Lady Diggleton was about to leave
when the editor leaned in once more.
"One more thing, Lady Diggleton.
Tomorrow's paper will reveal that there
is a thief in Mayfair, so do be careful."

"A thief?" Lady Diggleton said. "How
awful."

"Indeed, and whoever it is has very
particular taste, especially in jewelry,
so keep your windows and doors locked
tight."

"I most assuredly will, Mr. Tippletattle. Thank you for your kind assistance."

"Anytime, Lady Diggleton!"

A thief? Penelope thought as they left the building and turned toward Puggleton Park. *That sounds most unpleasant!* She would have to make sure their home was safe each night before she went to bed. This was just as well, as Penelope already checked the kitchen each night for Dreadful Squirrel. One never knew when he might attempt to steal his favorite dessert.

I do hope nobody tries to steal anything from us, she thought. *For although I'm just a pug, my bark can be quite loud indeed!*

CHAPTER THREE

Lady Diggleton and Penelope were settling down for tea when her footman entered the drawing room with a cream-colored card on a tray.

"Thank you, George," said Lady Diggleton, reaching for the card.

"You're most welcome, Lady Diggleton," George replied.

"Who do you think this could be from?" Lady Diggleton asked Penelope

as she turned the card over to read it.
Penelope watched as her eyes grew
wide, then she suddenly said, "Oh my!
How splendid!"

"Did something happen, Lady Diggleton?" Abby asked as she entered the room.

Lady Diggleton was about to read the invitation aloud when suddenly Lady Picklebottom appeared in the doorway, her bright yellow dress blinding in the afternoon sunlight.

"I HAVE JUST RECEIVED THE MOST INCREDIBLE INVITATION!" she said at the top of her voice.

"I believe both of us have," said Lady Diggleton.

Lady Picklebottom plucked the card from Lady Diggleton's hand and compared it to a card of her own.

"YES!" she said, overwhelmed with excitement. "THESE ARE THE VERY SAME!"

The very same what? thought Penelope, placing her front paws on Lady Diggleton's knees to convey the urgency of her curiosity.

"Why don't you read it aloud, Lady Picklebottom?"

"I believe I shall!" She began . . .

By Command of the Queen,

Lady Diggleton and her delightful pug shall
report to Windsor Castle to receive the
Order of the British Empire for
her good works with the Ladies' Society
for the Relief of Lost Dogs.

The ceremonies shall involve two days
of frolicking and celebration,
beginning on the seventh of June.

Signed,
Her Majesty, the Queen of England

"Heavenly biscuits!" Abby exclaimed.
"You are to stay with the Queen?"

"YES, YES!" said Lady Picklebottom,
jumping up and down. "WE ARE
BOTH INVITED TO STAY WITH THE
QUEEN AND RECEIVE A SPECIAL
AWARD FOR OUR CHARITY!"

Her elation finally exhausted her, and Lady Picklebottom sank into a chair while fanning her face.

"Now," said Lady Picklebottom, "as your oldest friend I must speak to you, Lady Diggleton. I have always had reason to compliment you on your manners, but I fear you are not prepared for an engagement as important as this. After all, it is the Queen who determines one's place in society."

"But I'm not concerned about my place in society," said Lady Diggleton.

"Nonsense," Lady Picklebottom said. "Fortunately for us both, I am well schooled in etiquette, and know all the rules one uses when visiting the Queen!" She turned to look at the little pug. "Isn't that right, Penelope?"

Penelope stared back. She didn't think there was anything wrong with her Lady's manners. Lady Picklebottom's, on the other hand . . .

"I don't recall you ever staying with the Queen," Lady Diggleton said.

"I have not had the honor," said Lady Picklebottom, "but one must be prepared! Now, if you and Penelope would rise, I shall teach you everything you need to know about staying with Her Majesty.

"When you meet the Queen you must curtsy—never bow. Please, demonstrate your abilities."

In response, Lady Diggleton performed a perfect curtsy, while Penelope bent her head with her paws forward, as she'd been taught to do.

"NOT LIKE THAT!" Lady Picklebottom yelled, startling them both so much that Lady Diggleton almost toppled a nearby bouquet.

"Lower your head! Put your right foot behind your left! Take the edges of your dress and pull them out just so! Bend your knees! And lower yourself, to show that you are a most lowly person indeed, while the Queen is the most important person who ever lived!" Lady Picklebottom demonstrated, then said, "Again."

Lady Diggleton and Penelope repeated their curtsies with little alteration.

"That was much improved," said Lady Picklebottom. "But practice as though your life depends upon it,

because it likely does! Now, the second most important thing—you shall *never* refer to the Queen as 'Your Majesty' after you have greeted her for the first time. You shall then only refer to the Queen in person as 'ma'am.' And never speak to Her Majesty before you have been spoken to. If she eats, you must eat. But if she does not eat, you still must eat, or you will insult the chef's cooking! If she stands to leave the room, stand to show your respect but do not follow unless asked. And *never* touch Her Majesty, even if she is about to trip or fall."

"But surely that can't be right," said Lady Diggleton.

"Indeed it is!" Lady Picklebottom said. "Better a cracked knee than a breach in etiquette!" She took a deep breath. "This instruction is tiring, especially with unstudied students. But, if you like, I shall review everything once more—"

"No need!" said Lady Diggleton. "You have taught us well, my friend." She began walking Lady Picklebottom to the door. "Now surely you must get home to pack. We are to stay at the palace for two days, after all."

"You are right," said Lady Picklebottom. "To think that just by helping dogs I would get invited to Windsor Castle. Goodness knows I've been trying to get such an invitation for years!"

That night, Abby helped Lady

Diggleton get ready for bed, while Penelope lay on the rug before the fire.

Abby brushed Lady Diggleton's dark hair in long strokes and frowned.

"Is something wrong, Abby?" asked Lady Diggleton.

Abby hesitated. "It is just Lady Picklebottom . . . she is a bit . . . overbearing, at times, is she not? Saying you need minding when it comes to your manners. Preposterous!"

Lady Diggleton laughed. "Lady Picklebottom can be bold when it comes to her opinions, it's true. But I believe certain friendships can be so valuable that one must allow for differences in personality. We have known one another since we were children, after all."

Abby nodded. "You are a true friend, Lady Diggleton. I wish you a good night."

"Good night, Abby."

From her spot near the crackling fire, Penelope pondered their exchange. *What would it be like,* she wondered, *to have a friend of my own? Lady Diggleton is my best friend, of course, but what if I had a canine friend? Could there be a dog with whom I could share a special bond?*

As Moon rose in the night sky, Penelope found herself making a wish for a new friend. *A fellow dog to play with and confide in,* she thought, *would truly make life complete.*

CHAPTER FOUR

After two days of fussing and packing and primping, Penelope, Lady Diggleton, and Lady Picklebottom watched as George and Abby piled their luggage high upon their carriage.

Once the happy trio were settled inside, the horses nickered and the carriage began its journey through the streets of London.

"Isn't this glorious?" said Lady

Picklebottom, who brought so many
bags with her that some of them were
on the seat beside her.

"It is indeed," said Lady Diggleton. "I believe Penelope is enjoying the ride as well, aren't you, Penelope?"

Penelope wagged her tail as she stuck her head out the window.

"Please tell me we are not going to sit here and talk to the dog all day," Lady Picklebottom said.

Lady Diggleton laughed. "I promise we shall not. Although I daresay I enjoy speaking with Penelope more than I do most people."

The swaying carriage was making
Penelope tired, so she curled up in the
lap of her dear Lady. *There is nothing
like the rocking of a carriage to induce
the loveliest of naps,* she thought. *And I,
for one, find them . . .* But she was sound
asleep before she could finish the
thought!

"Penelope," Lady Diggleton said. "It
is time to awaken, my dear. Windsor
Castle is just ahead."

Penelope opened her eyes, shook her head to wake herself, and gazed out the window. An enormous castle came into view, its turrets and chimneys gleaming in stark relief against the pale blue sky.

How could the journey be over so soon? she thought. *It seems as though we just left home moments ago.*

Little did she know that her journey was far from over, for there are not only journeys from here to there, but also journeys of the heart, which can take longer and are often far more interesting.

CHAPTER FIVE

The carriage pulled into a great arched entryway, and Lady Diggleton, Lady Picklebottom, and Penelope got out. A heavy oak door opened, and there stood none other than Mr. Weeby, England's most well-known dog trainer!

"Greetings, my ladies, greetings," he said. "Welcome to Windsor Castle."

"Whatever are you doing here,

Mr. Weeby?" said Lady Diggleton.

"Please, follow me and I shall explain while I bring you to the Queen."

Lady Diggleton and Lady Picklebottom exchanged glances. The Queen wanted to see them this instant?

As though he could read their minds, Mr. Weeby said, "If she is not otherwise detained, the Queen prefers to meet her guests at the soonest possible moment."

Penelope, Lady Diggleton, and Lady Picklebottom followed him into a stone entrance hall that was lit with torches. At the far end, a wide staircase led them to the rooms above.

"I believe I may have mentioned that I train Her Majesty's dog, Duchess," Mr. Weeby said. "And while I would not say that I am the only person in England who could do so properly, I have heard others say it once or twice."

He turned into the picture gallery, which was filled with painted portraits of queens and kings with their most beloved of dogs.

"As for why I am here at precisely this time, let me say that Duchess has been experiencing certain . . . difficulties. Not because I did anything wrong with my training, of course. That would be impossible."

"What sort of difficulties?" asked Lady Diggleton.

"Oh, you know, the sort that . . . ahem . . . a dog can have. Now look at this room! Is it not glorious?" he said, changing the subject.

The room was grand indeed, festooned with gold from floor to ceiling and rich red carpeting as far as the eye could see. Lady Picklebottom seemed to be most impressed, for she could not stop saying, "Lovely! Oh my, how very lovely!"

But what captivated Penelope most were the chandeliers. They were ten times the size of the ones she adored at Lady Diggleton's and blinked like impossible balls of starlight.

"Ah, we have arrived," said Mr. Weeby as they reached a pair of tall golden doors. "Of course, you have met the Queen before, Lady Diggleton, on the night of the Begood Ball, which, may I say, was one of my greatest triumphs!"

"I have," said Lady Diggleton, "but only for a brief moment."

They were about to step forward when Penelope was suddenly overcome. The castle was most intimidating, and she pulled back on her leash, thinking, *This is all too grand. It is simply too much.*

"Just a moment, Mr. Weeby," said Lady Diggleton, kneeling. "Are you afraid, my darling pug?" she asked softly, stroking Penelope's soft fur. "I admit that I am rather anxious myself. But there are times when we must face our fears. For then we may find them to be not quite as terrifying as we first believed."

Hearing her Lady's calming words, Penelope stopped panting and tried to arrange herself with the most dignity she could muster. Lady Diggleton smiled and nodded to Mr. Weeby. They were ready.

The doors opened, and twenty paces ahead appeared the Queen sitting upon a golden throne, more magnificent than ever. Her pale blue dress was studded with pearls, while a diamond ring on her left hand dazzled in the sunlight. Next to the Queen was Duchess, Her Majesty's King Charles spaniel, who sat regally on a tuffet with her black-and-tan coat agleam and a shimmering, bejeweled collar around her neck. Behind them both stood a sniffling man whose nose was so crimson that it matched his red uniform.

"Come forward," the Queen commanded.

Lady Diggleton, Lady Picklebottom, and Penelope crossed the room, and when they were close enough to smell the Queen's perfume, they curtsied.

There was a long silence as the Queen studied their form. Then she said, "You may rise," just as the man behind her let out a most enormous sneeze—*achoo!*

Lady Diggleton, Penelope, and Lady Picklebottom were all startled. The Queen, however, looked most annoyed and said, "Captain Clutterbeak, you must desist your constant sneezing!"

The captain wiped his nose with a handkerchief and said, "I shall try, ma'am—*achoo!*"

With a roll of her eyes, she turned back to her guests. "The captain of my royal guard, Captain Clutterbeak, sneezes almost as much as he breathes." She paused. "Nevertheless, may I welcome you to Windsor Castle. I am quite impressed by your Ladies' Society for the Relief of Lost Dogs. I'm told you have raised a lot of funds."

"Thank you, ma'am," said Lady Diggleton, while a nervous Lady Picklebottom, who rarely if ever kept her thoughts to herself, could find nothing to say.

"How many dogs have you placed in new homes thus far?" the Queen asked.

"One hundred and eight, ma'am," said Lady Diggleton.

"Well done. We shall have such fun celebrating your accomplishment. I daresay I remember meeting you and your pug the night of the Begood Ball. I was most impressed by her manners, and so I have decided that she shall be the Royal Canine Companion for Duchess over these next two days. My hope is that they will become good friends."

At this, Penelope's curiosity rose. *A friend?* she thought. *Oh, but this could be a most delightful circumstance!*

She looked at Duchess to see if she was similarly excited, but the spaniel was staring off into the distance, preoccupied by what, Penelope did not know.

Suddenly, everyone was startled

by another *achoo* from Captain Clutterbeak, which the Queen pretended not to notice. (Although she most certainly did.)

"Enough of these formalities," the Queen said, reaching into her pocket. She tossed one treat to Duchess and another to Penelope, who caught it in her mouth and gobbled it down before it hit the floor.

The Queen rang a bell. Mr. Weeby appeared in the doorway.

"Take Duchess and Penelope to the garden so they may get acquainted," commanded the Queen. "Ladies, my butler shall show you to your rooms. Dinner will commence at eight o'clock sharp."

The Queen turned to leave the room,

but before she did, she looked at Duchess and Penelope. "Behave, my dears," she said. "You would not like to know what happens to dogs who do not."

Penelope could not tell if she was joking or quite serious indeed.

CHAPTER SIX

Mr. Weeby led Duchess and Penelope to a green lawn near the kitchen gardens, where lettuce, pole beans, raspberries, and potatoes were grown for Her Majesty.

"Well," Mr. Weeby said, looking down at both dogs, "as Her Majesty has commanded, you two shall now become friends."

With that, he left!

So Penelope sat there, waiting for
Duchess to speak. But Duchess merely
looked in the opposite direction, as
though she saw something fascinating
in the nearby trees.

Am I supposed to speak to Duchess, or wait until she speaks to me? Penelope wondered, for she knew that there were very strict rules when it came to who spoke first with the Queen.

But soon the silence stretched on until Penelope could tolerate it no more.

"Mr. Weeby can be quite funny, can he not?" she said.

There was a pause as Duchess turned to look at her with a haughty gaze. "I hadn't noticed," she said.

"Well, he spoke as though friendship should begin with a royal decree," Penelope said, laughing a little. "While I believe, despite my limited experience, that attachments don't often start by command from the Queen of England."

"What, pray tell, is wrong with commands from the Queen of England?"

"Oh, nothing, it's just—"

"That you would sooner disobey Her Majesty than become friends with me?"

"Of course not," Penelope said, getting confused.

"Perhaps I shall tell you what I find humorous. I find it humorous that a dog who, I have heard, was once a stray in Puggleton Park could think that she could qualify as an acquaintance of mine. I also believe it's humorous that you dare speak to me before I have spoken to you, as that is a breach in royal etiquette. Not that I expect someone with so little stature to understand such things—after the death of her husband, your lady hardly qualifies as a person of stature herself."

Penelope bristled at this insult to Lady Diggleton. "I think you misunderstand," she said, a bite of anger in her voice.

"I misunderstand nothing," interrupted Duchess, her collar glittering in the afternoon sunlight. "You don't belong here, and neither does your lady."

Penelope was astonished, and her mouth hung open like she'd been slapped by a cold fish. She had never met a dog nor a human as rude as Duchess in her life.

"How dare you!" she sputtered.

"I do not mean to offend you," said Duchess. "I am simply stating the truth."

Penelope was speechless as the spaniel walked away with her nose high in the air. *Why, that is the most arrogant dog I have ever had the displeasure to meet,* she thought. *And to think she would speak of my dear Lady Diggleton in such a way—that was most contemptible!*

She sat upon the grass, angry and bewildered. How could a dog be so contemptuous toward her? Even a royal one? It was absolutely ridiculous!

Suddenly a large shadow loomed above her. Startled, Penelope turned and saw two cows—one black and white, and one all black.

"What is wrong with youuu?" the black cow mooed.

Penelope did not feel like talking,

but she knew she should be polite.
"Nothing, I assure you," she said.

"I am Miss Greenstalk," the black-and-white cow said, then gestured to her friend. "This is Miss Berrycloth."

"I'm Penelope," the little pug said, eager for the conversation to be over so she could brood in peace. "Pleased to make your acquaintance."

"We saw youuu with Duchess, Her Majesty's dog," said Miss Berrycloth.

"Yes, and what of it?" Penelope asked, her bad mood getting the better of her.

"Nooo dogs get along with her," said Miss Greenstalk.

"And we do mean *nooo* dogs," said Miss Berrycloth.

"Is that true?" Penelope asked.

The cows nodded their great heads.

"The Queen invites neeew dogs to come and play," said Miss Greenstalk, leaning forward as though she did not mind a bit of gossip when it came her way. "But the neeew canine always vows never to return."

Miss Berrycloth nodded. "We heard that one dog did his business in the Crimson Drawing Rooom to ensure he would never be asked back."

Both cows giggled, for that was surely a scandal.

"How do you know all this?" Penelope asked.

"The mice," said Miss Berrycloth. "They are gossips of the wooorst kind."

Penelope nodded. "Indeed. So, Duchess has no friends at all?"

"Nooo," mooed the cows.

"Well," Penelope said, deciding that she liked Miss Berrycloth and Miss Greenstalk very much, "I should like to think of you both as newfound friends."

The cows nodded as Penelope heard Mr. Weeby calling her name.

"I apologize, but I must be going," Penelope said.

"See you sooon!" said Miss Berrycloth.

"And bring us neeews from the castle!" said Miss Greenstalk as Penelope ran off to find Lady Diggleton, one of the truest friends a dog could hope to have.

CHAPTER SEVEN

Mr. Weeby watched as Penelope approached him, quite alone.

"I see Duchess has left," he said with a sigh. "It seems not even a trainer of the highest stature can make her behave in a tolerable manner."

He gestured for Penelope to follow as he strode back into the castle.

Penelope thought about what the cows had told her as she trotted behind

Mr. Weeby through room after room.

"I do worry what I shall do if her bad behavior continues," Mr. Weeby muttered to himself.

"Of course, she's so spoiled that not even a trainer as skilled as myself can do a thing about it."

Mr. Weeby knocked at the entrance

to Lady Diggleton's bedchamber, and when she opened the door, he bid her a good afternoon and left without bragging about himself at all, which Penelope thought was a most unusual thing for him to do indeed.

"Did you enjoy your time with Duchess, dear Penelope?" asked Lady Diggleton as Penelope entered the room.

I did not, Penelope thought. *I found her to be most disagreeable.*

"Perhaps she could be a lasting friend," said Lady Diggleton.

Perhaps she is the last friend I could ever be prevailed upon to have, thought Penelope, throwing herself down upon the carpet with a sigh.

Lady Diggleton frowned. "Are you all right, my darling?"

She knelt down to get a better look at the little pug. "I daresay you seem quite low. I hope you didn't eat something that disagreed with you. Or is there something stuck in your paw?"

Lady Diggleton checked Penelope's paws and found nothing. She gently placed her upon the bed and scratched behind her left ear. "Have a rest, dear Penelope, for soon it will be dinner."

Dinner? thought Penelope, alarmed. *How on earth am I going to dine with that wretched dog?*

At precisely eight o'clock, Penelope and Lady Diggleton entered the great dining hall. A footman announced them at top volume, saying, "LADY

DIGGLETON AND PENELOPE THE PUG!"

The Queen approached in an elaborate gown that rustled as she walked. A tiara sat upon her head, while her diamond ring gleamed on her left hand. Behind her, a merry party sat around a gold table that was covered with flowers and candles. "I am pleased you are here," she said. "Not that you have much say in the matter," she added with a crisp laugh.

"Thank you for the kind invitation, ma'am," said Lady Diggleton.

"It is time for introductions. This is my brother, Prince James of Yorkieshire," she said as a handsome man with mussed brown hair bowed his head.

"Pleased to make your acquaintance," he said.

"And this is Lady Shivvers, my lady-in-waiting." A woman with frizzy blond hair tucked tightly into a bun attempted a nervous smile.

"You know Lady Picklebottom and Mr. Weeby, of course," said the Queen.

"And you remember the head of my royal guard, Captain Clutterbeak."

The captain gave a stern nod before releasing an *achoo!* that made everyone at the table jump.

"So pleased to meet you all," said Lady Diggleton as an attendant pulled out her chair. She reached down to lift Penelope onto her lap when the Queen interrupted.

"Penelope and Duchess shall dine at the dogs' table," she said, motioning to a corner where gold bowls lay on a small table.

"What do you think, Penelope?" Lady Diggleton asked.

Realizing she didn't have much choice, Penelope gave a small wag so her Lady would not worry, then walked toward her place, where Duchess was already seated. *I wonder what sort of reception I will receive,* Penelope thought. But because she was an optimistic dog, she began to think that maybe there was a way to improve the situation.

Perhaps Duchess and I have gotten off on the wrong paw, she thought. *If that is the case, then I should try again, for only a fool would rather have a foe than a friend.*

Penelope took her place before a golden bowl that was filled to the brim with cuts of meat and roast potatoes.

"Hello," she said to Duchess. "How are you this evening?"

"I was quite well until just now," said Duchess, without looking up from her dinner.

Of course, that was a rather rude reply, but Penelope decided she would not be deterred so easily. "I so enjoy roast chicken," she said, swallowing a particularly tasty morsel. "And may I say the preparation here at Windsor is the best I've ever had?"

As if in reply, Duchess turned her snout away from the chicken in her bowl and ate a potato instead.

"It is your turn to speak," Penelope said, trying to remain polite even though Duchess had been horribly rude thus far. "I talked about the food, now you could talk about the weather."

"Do you always talk while you eat?" said Duchess.

"I do when there is someone pleasant to talk to," said Penelope.

"Then I shall try to be as unpleasant as possible. I must confess I prefer to dine by myself when the Queen will allow me to do so."

"Do you find all company undesirable?"

"If it is anyone but the Queen, yes. And if it is a dog who smells like a farm hound, I find company most undesirable indeed."

Penelope felt her temper rise just as it had earlier in the day, but it would not do to growl and snap at the Queen's companion. *I tried my best to make peace with Duchess, but she clearly doesn't want my friendship*, Penelope thought, realizing that she'd rather skip dinner than spend one more moment in the Royal canine's company.

"Allow me to let you dine alone, since that is what you prefer," Penelope said. "I daresay I have suddenly lost my appetite."

Of course, Penelope was in fact very hungry, because she is a dog, and dogs do not like to skip dinner at all. Nevertheless, she tried to ignore her grumbling tummy as she walked back to the large table and lay at her Lady's feet. *I had to walk away*, she thought. *I deserve better treatment than that, not only from a potential friend, but from anyone.*

Penelope wasn't paying much attention when Lady Picklebottom complimented the Queen on her enormous ring. The ring was set with the Canis Diamond, which was believed to be one of the largest precious jewels in the world. Prince James remarked that their father, the former King, told them that the stone was cursed.

"Cursed?" asked Lady Diggleton.

"Yes," said Lady Shivvers, who trembled at the thought. "The story is that the diamond was stolen from its rightful owner years ago, and it will take revenge upon anyone who wears it."

"Utter nonsense!" said the Queen. "The Canis Diamond has been in my family for hundreds of years. Now"— she turned to the butler—"it's time to serve my pastry chef's famous raspberry tarts."

The butler frowned as an attendant whispered in his ear.

"I'm afraid there are no tarts this evening, ma'am," he said.

"What?" she said. "How can there be no raspberry tarts?"

"We found scratch marks on the baskets where the tarts were kept, ma'am, along with tangles of fur."

"Rats, no doubt!" said the Queen. "Such horrid little creatures. Of course," she added, "all the best castles have them."

As the humans talked about what they should have for dessert, Penelope nodded off to sleep, completely unaware that she should have listened to the tale of the Canis Diamond, for something rather shocking was going to happen—and soon.

CHAPTER EIGHT

Penelope was awakened by a symphony of sounds that rumbled and gurgled, blubbed and squelched. It was her empty stomach, of course, loudly protesting her decision to go to bed without dinner. As her eyes adjusted to the darkness, she realized that Lady Diggleton must have carried her up to her bedchamber after the meal. Her stomach gurgled again, this

time even more loudly than before. *Perhaps I can find something in the kitchen*, she thought. *There is often a tasty morsel or two on the floor at home.*

Lady Diggleton was breathing deeply as Penelope crept to the door and nudged it open with her nose. She stepped into the torchlit hallway and shivered.

The air was cold, and the stone floor even colder. Her paws made a clicking sound as she walked along, while the displays of armor loomed. She knew no one was inside them, of course, but they were upsetting just the same.

At long last she found the enormous kitchen. Pots and pans hung from the ceiling, and shelves groaned with dishes and crockery.

Penelope began searching the floor for crumbs when suddenly she smelled something familiar.

"What are you doing here?"

Penelope jumped as Duchess stepped out from a dark corner. "My goodness, you just gave me a fright," she said.

"If you're looking for scraps, there usually are but the floor has been thoroughly cleaned," said Duchess.

Penelope tried to hide her disappointment, and she refused to ask Duchess if there was any other food to be found. So instead she bid her goodnight and turned to leave, her stomach growling loudly.

Duchess frowned. *I am the reason the pug skipped her evening meal,* she thought. *And, in truth, she has not been as disagreeable as I thought she'd be . . .*

"Wait," she said. "I must admit I have been alarmed by your inferiority since you arrived at the castle. But I've realized that you are not quite so lowly as I at first believed. In fact, I think I can overlook your lack of social standing and abominable manners and offer you a friendship, of sorts. As long as we are never seen in public together, of course."

Penelope looked at the spaniel as if she couldn't believe her fuzzy black ears.

"My manners?" she said. "From the moment we met, your manners have been most monstrous indeed. You have done everything you could to convince me that you are arrogant, selfish, and do not care for the feelings of anyone who has the misfortune to make your acquaintance. So I will gladly turn down your offer of 'friendship,' which is a concept you don't seem to understand in the slightest. Good night."

Duchess was about to reply when suddenly a loud scream came from somewhere deep in the castle. Then, whoever it was screamed again!

Penelope tried to keep up with Duchess as she raced toward the sound. The castle was enormous, but Duchess knew exactly where she was going. The dogs skidded around a corner and up a long corridor. Then they raced up two flights of slippery stone stairs. Penelope found it almost impossible to keep up, but she would not allow herself to lose sight of the Royal canine out of fear that Lady Diggleton could be in danger. Just as Penelope thought she could run no more, Duchess dashed past two guards and into the Queen's bedchamber.

Captain Clutterbeak was already

inside, asking the Queen if she was all right.

"I most certainly am not," she replied. "Captain! My ring—and the Canis Diamond—is gone!" She motioned to a vanity where the ring was meant to be.

"But, ma'am, are you saying"—the captain sneezed most violently—"that you did not send the ring to the castle vault for the night?"

"I did not," the Queen said, eyeing him with distaste as he blew his nose, "as I intended to wear it again tomorrow. After all, there are two guards at my door, as you can plainly see, and the window is far too high up for any human being to climb through. I assumed the guards were keeping my ring quite safe. Apparently, I was wrong."

As the Queen spoke, the prince, along with Lady Diggleton and Lady Picklebottom, appeared. "What happened?" said the prince.

"Is the Queen safe?" asked Lady Diggleton, noticing Penelope, who somehow had arrived in the Queen's room before her.

"She is quite safe," the captain said, convulsing with yet another tremendous *achoo!* "But it is most unsatisfactory to have so many people gathered here. The guards will see you into the drawing room as I conduct a thorough inspection. And wake the others," he said to the guards. "I should like to speak to them as—*ah-ah-achoo!*—as well."

"Yes, Captain," a guard replied, trying not to react as his face was misted with the captain's spittle.

The captain turned toward the Queen. "May I suggest that you go with them, ma'am?" He sniffled. "I do believe you will be more comfortable there, perhaps with a cup of tea?"

"That is thoughtful of you, Captain," replied the Queen, picking up Duchess and holding her close for comfort. "But I shall expect a full report—and soon."

It wasn't long before everyone was gathered downstairs. Penelope sat on Lady Diggleton's lap, while Duchess sat with the Queen. The clock struck midnight as Lady Picklebottom and Lady Shivvers sipped their tea, with nothing but the sound of a ticking clock to keep them company.

"It seems our plan to celebrate the Ladies' Society for the Relief of Lost Dogs has been upended by this shocking crime," said the Queen.

"The safety of your person and

property is so much more important," said Lady Diggleton.

The Queen nodded, looking most upset indeed.

Thirty long minutes passed until the captain entered the room.

"Have you found anything?" the Queen said.

"I have," he said. "But first I have some questions for you. *Achoo!*" The Queen flinched, looking most annoyed as he wiped his nose, which seemed to grow more crimson by the minute. "Pardon me, ma'am."

"You may desist saying 'Pardon me, ma'am' every time you sneeze!" said the Queen. "You do so constantly, so clearly I have pardoned you many times already."

"Yes, ma'am." The captain cleared his throat. "You sleep with your window open, is that correct?"

"I prefer the fresh air," she replied.

He nodded and turned to the Prince of Yorkieshire and Lady Shivvers. "Pardon me for asking, Sir, but where were you during the time of the robbery?"

"I was with Lady Shivvers, warming myself before the drawing room fire," the prince replied as the nervous lady nodded.

The captain looked to Mr. Weeby. "Has everyone on the staff been accounted for?"

Mr. Weeby hesitated and said, "In a situation such as this, I must flatter myself and say that I am an honest man.

Which is why I must tell you that the staff and I were in the lower quarters playing cards at the time of the robbery."

"You play card games in my castle?" the Queen said with surprise.

"I'm afraid so, ma'am," said Mr. Weeby, looking most embarrassed.

"Then I have reached a shocking but most logical conclusion," said the captain. "Whoever stole the Canis Diamond—*sniffle, sniffle, achoo!*—is right here in this very room!"

Everyone exchanged shocked glances, including Penelope and Duchess, who could not help but meet one another's gaze in surprise.

The captain strode to the center of the room, relishing the moment. "Before I name the thief, allow me to present the evidence I've collected," he said. "The robbery took place at precisely ten past eleven this evening. How do I know? Because that is when the Queen's clock, which was placed on the vanity with the ring, was knocked over and smashed. It was not broken before then, ma'am?"

"It was not," the Queen said.

"Exactly as I suspected," said the captain. "At the same time, the prince and Lady Shivvers were together enjoying a fire, so we can rule them both out as the thief. Meanwhile, Mr. Weeby and the staff were all playing cards downstairs, so they are all accounted for. Also, I have guards who walk the halls each night, and they have assured me that Lady

Diggleton and Lady Picklebottom were in their bedchambers before the Queen screamed. In fact, there was only *one* of us who was not where they were supposed to be. And that is . . . Duchess!"

If ever a dog had the expression of *"Who, me?!"* on its face, it was the spaniel, who looked most startled indeed.

"Captain," the Queen said. "Do tell me you are not implying that *my dog* stole the Canis Diamond? For that would be the most ridiculous thing I have ever heard in my life."

"I realize it may sound that way, ma'am," said the captain, letting out a blast of sneezes. "But may I ask where Duchess was when you awoke to find your ring gone?"

"No, this cannot be," said the Queen. "I do not remember seeing my darling Duchess at all!" She paused as Duchess, still in her lap, began to look increasingly alarmed. "But there are the guards at my door! Surely they would have noticed Duchess leaving my bedchamber!"

One of the guards stepped forward. "I apologize, ma'am, but Duchess often leaves your bedchamber at night."

"Do you not stop her?"

"We're too scared, ma'am," the other guard said sheepishly. "She once bit my finger. It was most uncomfortable, and I bled!"

The captain cleared his throat with a wet gargle that sounded like *grughumhum*. "If I may continue," he said. "The Queen's vanity had scratch marks along the top, which could only have been made by an animal's claws." He let that sink in a moment.

"But even more importantly, that's where I found the clumps of black-and-tan fur, along with this!"

Everyone gasped as he pulled Duchess's collar out of his pocket and handed it to the Queen.

Before anyone could speak, or even move, Duchess leaped off the Queen's lap and made a desperate scramble for the door.

"Stop her!" the captain said, and two guards ran after the little dog.

But Duchess was hard to catch. She ran behind a sofa, under a table, and almost made her escape when she ran between the captain's legs. But it was no good. Duchess was caught before she reached the door, and the Queen watched in desperation as a guard picked her up and held her tight.

"No!" the Queen said, tears filling her eyes. "But this is too horrible!"

"I know this must be difficult, but my only remaining question is where the Royal canine put the ring, ma'am," the captain said gently. "I will begin the search immediately. Upon my honor, we shall take good care of Duchess until her transfer to the Home for Wayward Dogs in the morning."

"But this simply can't be," said the

Queen, tears sparkling in her eyes.

The captain nodded. "I am confident that once you have had time to consider the evidence, you will realize that the thief, as painful as it may be, is, in fact, your dog."

He motioned to the guards, and they carried Duchess away as everyone, including Penelope, watched in dismay.

CHAPTER NINE

Perhaps you are wondering, as Penelope was, what Duchess would do with a ring? Or, better yet, what *any* dog would do with one?

Or perhaps, like Penelope, you are very clever, and have figured out that the thief could not have been Duchess at all.

I was with Duchess in the kitchen when the Queen screamed! thought Penelope.

Then we ran to her quarters together, as sure as can be!

Penelope looked at Lady Diggleton with the utmost urgency. Could she not see that a most terrible error had been made? In an attempt to make her Lady understand, the little pug whimpered, then pawed at the sleeve of her dress.

"My dear Penelope!" Lady Diggleton said. "I can see you are most distressed.

Of course, this evening has been most upsetting for us all," she said.

Penelope did not know what to do, for she could not tell her Lady that Duchess was innocent; Lady Diggleton was not fluent in dog!

"I believe it is time for us all to return to bed," Lady Picklebottom said. "We won't know anything more until the morning, and I imagine everyone is most tired—especially you, ma'am."

The Queen, wiping tears from her eyes, nodded. "Captain Clutterbeak is convinced my dog is the culprit," she said, "and if that is true, I have no choice but to send her to the Home for Wayward Dogs."

"Surely you can make an exception," said Lady Diggleton.

The Queen shook her head. "Our laws apply to everyone, I'm afraid. Even Duchess."

She looked at the hand where her ring usually sat. "My father always said the Canis Diamond was cursed. I never believed him until tonight."

The humans returned to bed, hoping that some new explanation would be found in the morning. But as Lady Diggleton slept fitfully, Penelope lay awake, tormented by her thoughts. She found Duchess to be most disagreeable, to be sure, but no dog should be punished for a crime they did not commit.

She looked out the window and was gladdened to see her friend Moon hanging high in the sky.

"What shall I do?" Penelope asked Moon.

"What shall you do?" Moon replied.

"That is what I am asking you, my friend," she said. "What shall I do?"

"And that is what I am saying in return," said Moon. "What shall *you* do?"

Penelope realized that Moon was making a point.

"You are saying that I must decide for myself," she replied.

"I am," said Moon. "For the most courageous acts do not come from the advice of a friend, they come from the depths of a hero's heart."

Penelope thought a moment. "Perhaps I have the beginnings of a plan in place," she said. "But first I must find Duchess."

Moon glimmered, which meant she was pleased with Penelope's answer. The little pug bowed her head in respect. "Thank you, Moon," she said. "You have never steered me off course."

But how would she find Duchess? The castle held over a thousand rooms. She wondered who could possibly know where Duchess was being held, and then she realized she knew exactly where to go.

Penelope crept as quickly but

as silently as she could from Lady Diggleton's bedchamber, then looked both ways to ensure there were no guards in the hall.

As she ran along, the empty armor of knights long gone surrounded her once more, but this time Penelope refused to be frightened. *Sometimes one's duty must outweigh their fears,* she thought. *Otherwise nothing of real importance would ever get done.*

Up ahead, she saw an arched doorway that led to the main field at the center of the castle. She dashed out into the darkness and ran until she could smell the warm scent of hay and dung. This was how she found Miss Berrycloth and Miss Greenstalk, who were sleeping with their herd.

First, Penelope tried to wake them by scratching at their hooves, which did not work. Then she tried nipping at their legs, which did not work. Finally, she pulled at their tails with her teeth, which worked wonderfully well indeed.

"What are youuu doing?" mooed Miss Berrycloth in alarm.

"I am most sorry to wake you," said Penelope, "but I fear there is an emergency."

"Youuu mean Duchess?" mooed Miss Greenstalk with a yawn. "She is in a great deal of danger."

"But I am certain she did not commit the crime," said Penelope.

"Hooow can you be sooo certain?" said Miss Berrycloth.

"Because she was with me."

"Hooow delightful!" said Miss Greenstalk.

"I need to know where the guards have taken her. Do you know?"

"Of course we knooow," said Miss Greenstalk. "She is being held in the

Rooound Tower. We saw the guards take her there with our ooown eyes."

Both cows looked at the Round Tower, and Penelope followed their gaze.

"Thank youuu. I mean, you," she said. "And wish me good fortune."

"We most certainly dooo," said the cows.

The enormous Round Tower was frightening to behold. Set in the midst of the great lawn, it was meant to defend the king or queen when the castle was under attack. Unfortunately, the tower also made for an excellent prison.

Feeling ever so exposed, Penelope crept forward on her belly. There were two guards at the door of the tower, both well-armed with spears and swords. She studied them in a panic. How could she possibly get past? She simply had no idea, so she decided to wait. *If one does not know what to do, it is usually best to do nothing,* she thought.

Have you ever found that if you do nothing long enough, you find the solution to the problem at hand? This is what happened to Penelope. The guards, she realized, had barely moved since she got there. In fact, they were leaning heavily upon the tower walls and breathing quite deeply. They were not guarding the tower, she realized; they were asleep!

Penelope cautiously approached. Neither of the guards moved. When she got closer, she spied something in the hand of one of the guards—a large iron ring, from which dangled a single key. *You can do this,* she said to herself. She carefully picked up the ring in her teeth and, scared the guard would awaken at any moment, slid it out of his grasp.

I've got it! she thought as she turned to creep into the tower and started to make her way up the stone staircase.

After much huffing and puffing, she reached the top and saw a cell with iron bars. The torchlight revealed a most unhappy dog indeed.

Nevertheless, seeing Penelope, Duchess sat upright as though she was still in the throne room on her royal tuffet. "What are *you* doing here?" she said.

"I am here to help you," Penelope replied.

"Why would you do that?" Duchess said, eyeing her with suspicion. "There is no friendship between us, as you made abundantly clear."

Penelope looked to the ceiling in frustration. "That may be true," she said, "but you are innocent, and I am the only one who knows it."

Duchess thought a moment. "Well, you have come in vain. I do not need your assistance."

"Your stubborn pride is going to get you sent to the Home for Wayward Dogs," said Penelope. "Do you not see that?"

Duchess did not reply, so Penelope turned to go back the way she came.

"Wait," Duchess said. "I shall accept your assistance just this once. But tell me—how do you expect to unlock this cell?"

Penelope looked at the lock and realized it was far too high for her to reach. For a moment she panicked, but then she saw a nearby chair.

Pushing it with her snout, she moved the chair next to the iron gate. Then

she climbed atop it and, with the key
in her teeth, slid it into the lock ever so
carefully. Both dogs held their breath
as she attempted to turn it. There was
a click, and they rejoiced as the door
swung open so Duchess could step out
of her cell.

"I feel that I must be clear," said Duchess as she stepped out of the cell. "Although I thank you for your assistance, this changes nothing between us."

"Please, do not make me regret that I rescued you," Penelope replied.

They made their way back to the entrance to the tower, where both guards were still asleep.

"The Queen's guards are paying attention as usual I see," Duchess muttered.

"Could you please be quiet?" said Penelope.

"You're the one speaking."

"Only because *you* were speaking!"

"And you are—awake!" Duchess shrieked. "The guards are awake!"

Not a moment passed before one of
the guards spotted them and shouted,
"Halt in the name of the Queen!"

"Run!" cried Penelope.

They raced across the great lawn
with Duchess leading the way as the
guards chased close behind. Duchess
swerved to the left, then right, then
ducked through a dark doorway into
the castle, but the guards remained

near at hand. In fact, no matter how
many twists and turns the dogs made,
the guards were unshakable. How
would they ever get away?

Duchess rounded a corner and
skidded to a halt. They were in a grand
library that appeared to have no exit,
save the one they'd just run through.

"What have you done?" Penelope
said. "There's no place to escape!"

"Give me a moment," Duchess said, jumping at a torch far overhead.

"But the guards—they're almost here!"

Duchess jumped again and hit the torch with her nose. Suddenly, a large bookshelf swung open to reveal a dark tunnel.

Penelope looked at Duchess in astonishment.

"One cannot have a castle without a secret passageway," Duchess said as she stepped inside. "Are you coming?"

"I am!" said Penelope.

The bookcase swung shut behind her, and not a moment too soon.

"Are you sure the guards don't know about this?" Penelope whispered, for she could already hear the guards searching the library.

"Nobody remembers this tunnel but me," said Duchess.

So, we are safe for the moment, Penelope thought, *but where does this passage lead? And what can I do to clear Duchess's name?*

CHAPTER TEN

Water dripped from the ceiling and echoed off the stone walls as Duchess and Penelope walked along the dirt floor.

"Where does this passage lead?"
Penelope asked.

"There is a fork not far ahead," said
Duchess. "One way leads to a swinging
portrait near the royal bedchambers,
the other leads to a tunnel that ends
deep in the woods. You shall take the
first, and I shall take the second."

"But you can't just run away!"

"I have no choice," said Duchess. "And neither does the Queen."

For the first time, Penelope realized how heartbroken Duchess really was. *She must love the Queen as much as I love my Lady*, she thought.

"There must be another way," Penelope said. "If you run, you will be a lone."

"How difficult could that be? You managed it after all."

For a moment, Penelope thought she should be offended, but then she realized that Duchess was making a joke. She could not resist a smile. "True, but before I found Lady Diggleton, the nights were bitter cold, and I longed for companionship. I would not wish the experience upon my worst enemy."

"I believe I *am* your worst enemy," Duchess said.

"Well, we can put that aside for the moment."

"We can certainly try."

Duchess stopped at the fork in the tunnel. "I must leave you here, for I see no other option."

"Wait," Penelope said. "If we can figure out who really stole the Canis Diamond, you will not have to run away and you can stay with the Queen."

Duchess shook her head. "Whoever framed me has done far too good a job. I must escape while I still can."

"But if we ask ourselves the right questions and follow the clues, wherever they may lead—"

"Two dogs, conducting an

investigation? Surely you don't believe we can prevail."

"I most certainly do. I may be just a pug, but I'm a rather clever one. And you may be just a spaniel, but you ..." Penelope trailed off.

"Trying to think of something nice to say?"

"... have a kind of stubbornness that will serve us well."

"For once I don't disagree," said Duchess. "However, if we have not found the real culprit by dawn, I will escape into the forest, no matter what you say."

Penelope nodded. "Then we are agreed."

While the dogs plotted their next

move, the Queen tossed and turned in her bed, unable to sleep. She could finally take it no longer, so she hurried to the Crimson Drawing Room and summoned Captain Clutterbeak.

When he arrived, she gave him her sternest look.

"Captain Clutterbeak, I simply do not believe that my dearest Duchess has stolen the Canis Diamond, no matter what your evidence indicates. I demand you bring her to me at once."

Captain Clutterbeak shook his head. "Ma'am, I assure you the dog is guilty, and the law is the law. You must not make a false decision due to your emotional state."

"Are you saying that I am 'emotional' when I make my judgments, Captain?

That I am not capable of making sound decisions while I not only run this castle but all of England?" the Queen said, her face flushing with anger. "Bring Duchess to me, now. This is a *command* from your Queen."

The color drained from Captain Clutterbeak's face, for he was about to reveal very bad news indeed.

"Th-that's not possible, ma'am."

"And why is that?"

"Because Duchess has escaped the Round Tower, with, it appears, Lady Diggleton's pug."

The very moment the words left his lips, Lady Diggleton rushed into the room. "Penelope is missing!" she exclaimed.

"I have just been informed that the

dogs are together," said the Queen, giving Captain Clutterbeak a withering look. "As for you, Captain, find those dogs or you shall suffer the mighty displeasure of your Queen."

The captain nodded and strode over to one of his guards. "Find that dog," he hissed, "and if she is with the pug, you know what to do. This ridiculousness must end tonight."

"Yes, Captain," the guard replied, leaving the room in great haste.

CHAPTER ELEVEN

The fake portrait swung open, and the dogs peered into the hall that led to the Queen's bedchambers. "Is the Queen in there?" Penelope asked.

"No," said Duchess. "There are no guards at the door."

"Then this is our chance to search her room for clues. Perhaps we will notice something the captain missed."

Duchess nodded and they entered the empty bedchamber, which somehow felt smaller without the Queen's presence.

"Let us go through our memories step by step," Penelope said. "The first thing I remember is running after you into the room."

"That's correct," said Duchess. "Captain Clutterbeak was already here."

"And where was he standing?" Penelope asked.

"He was over by the vanity where the gold box that held the Canis Diamond ring was kept."

Penelope paused a moment, deep in thought. "Who would want to frame you, do you think?"

"Who wouldn't? I'm not the most popular dog," said Duchess.

"That's certainly true," said Penelope. "But there's something else that's been bothering me. The captain had your collar. Do you remember losing it?"

"I didn't lose it," Duchess said. "I removed it."

"What?"

"That collar itches my neck most terribly at night. So, after the Queen goes to sleep, I slip it over my head and place it beside my bed. The following day, I put it back on."

"But how do you manage such a thing?" Penelope asked.

"I happen to have rather flexible ears and I'm quite a good wiggler."

Duchess pawed her ears until they both lay perfectly flat and wiggled along the floor to demonstrate. Penelope could not help but laugh, despite the dire circumstances.

"And yet, the captain said he found your collar on the vanity," Penelope said.

"You know, now that I think about it, I noticed that my collar was exactly where I'd left it the moment we entered the room."

"How can you be certain?" Penelope said.

"Because when the Queen said the Canis Diamond was gone, I looked to see if my collar was stolen, too, but it was still on the floor."

"This means the perpetrator moved it after we all left?" said Penelope.

Both dogs thought hard.

"Captain Clutterbeak told everyone to wait in the Crimson Drawing Room while he inspected the scene of the crime. He said he needed to be alone, did he not?" Penelope said.

"He did," said Duchess. "Which means the captain could've taken my collar—"

"—and slipped it into his pocket to present to the Queen as evidence against you!"

"Which would mean that Captain Clutterbeak framed me! And that means…"

The dogs looked at one another and spoke at the same time. *"Captain Clutterbeak stole the Canis Diamond!"*

They rejoiced for a moment, until Duchess said, "But we don't have the proof." Her tail sagged. "And without it, I am doomed."

When the dogs arrived at the captain's chambers, they were relieved to find it deserted. The sun was just peeking over the horizon while, through an open window, they heard guards calling their names. *"Penelope! Duchess!"*

"They are looking for us," Duchess said.

"If there is a clue to the captain's guilt," Penelope said, "I believe this is where we shall find it."

"You take the bed. I shall inspect the dresser."

Penelope started sniffing around the bed. "I can't find anything," she said.

"Nor can I," said Duchess, her face crumpling in despair. She looked out the window where a sliver of the sun was peeking over the horizon. "It's too late for me to escape," she said, "and I will spend the rest of my days in the Home for Wayward Dogs away from my beloved Queen." Duchess slumped onto her belly in defeat.

Suddenly, a ray of sunlight hit a dark corner of the room, and a glint of gold caught Duchess's eye. In a crouch, she scooted to a bureau and peered beneath. Duchess gasped.

"Did you find something?" Penelope said.

Duchess wiggled further under the bureau, grasped something with her mouth, and tugged it into the daylight.

"Look," Duchess said. "It's my grooming brush!

The captain must have removed my fur from it so he could show it to the Queen, then he hid it here so nobody would notice it was clean."

Penelope grinned. "That's the proof we need!"

"What should we do now?" Duchess said.

"The thing we do best," said Penelope.

Lady Diggleton, Lady Picklebottom, and the Queen were downstairs when they heard the dogs barking.

"It's Penelope and Duchess!" said Lady Diggleton.

"Let's go to them!" said the Queen.

They followed the barks to the captain's bedchamber and rushed in.

"Duchess!" cried the Queen, seeing her spaniel.

"Penelope!" cried Lady Diggleton, seeing her pug.

"Whose room is this?" cried Lady Picklebottom, who had followed them. "For it is not particularly tidy at all!"

"This is Captain Clutterbeak's

bedroom," said the Queen as she picked
up Duchess and held her close.

Lady Diggleton knelt to pick up
Penelope, but the pug was acting
most strangely, pacing to and fro,
whimpering the whole time.

"Did you find something, my dear?"
asked Lady Diggleton.

Penelope wagged her tail and
ran around behind Lady Diggleton,
pressing her cold nose to her ankles
and nudging her forward.

Duchess, meanwhile, wriggled out of the Queen's arms to run back and forth from the bureau to Her Majesty.

"My goodness!" said Lady Diggleton. "I believe there's something they want us to see."

"I do hope it's not a dead bird," said Lady Picklebottom. "I may care for dogs more than I once did, but I do not enjoy dead things as gifts."

Lady Diggleton walked toward the bureau where she saw the grooming brush on the floor. She picked it up and turned to the Queen.

"Do you recognize this?"

"It's Duchess's grooming brush," said the Queen, looking at it in confusion. "But who cleaned it? And why would the captain have it in his bedroom?"

Lady Diggleton and Lady Picklebottom looked at one another in confusion as the two dogs tried to contain themselves. *They're so close to figuring it out!* thought Penelope, bemoaning once again that the humans did not speak dog.

"I daresay, I believe I have an idea . . . ," said Lady Picklebottom.

"Please, Lady Picklebottom, now is not the time for you to prattle," said the Queen.

"This is not prattle, ma'am," said Lady Picklebottom. "What if the captain took the fur from the brush to frame Duchess, because he is the thief?"

The Queen eyed Lady Picklebottom, making her most nervous indeed, and then said, "That is a most interesting notion."

There was a sneeze, and they all turned to see Captain Clutterbeak standing in the doorway with two guards.

"Good morning, Captain," the Queen said. "Look at what the dogs found." She held up the gold brush.

"Oh—*achoo!*—that looks like a dog grooming brush," he sniffled.

"As I am well aware," said the Queen. "But what, pray tell, is it doing in your bedchamber?"

"In here? I—*ah*—I have no idea."

"I hope I do not sound 'emotional' when I say I don't believe you," said the Queen. "Especially since I keep this on my vanity."

Sweat beaded on the captain's forehead as he released another torrent of sneezes.

"But I'm telling the truth, ma'am! *Achoo!*"

"Captain, it is clear to me that you framed Duchess and stole my diamond ring. I demand to know where it is at once!"

"I don't have it! *Ah—ah*—I swear—*achoo*!" the captain said. "Please believe me, ma'am. It"—he sniffled again—"it wasn't me!"

The Queen narrowed her eyes. "If you tell me where the ring is, Captain, I shall merely send you to the Confinement for Calamitous Captains. If you do not, I will banish you from England forever."

"But—*ah-achoo*—I don't know! Why would I frame Duchess? *Ah-ah-I* wouldn't, I swear upon my life!"

"May I ask the captain a question?" Lady Diggleton said.

"You may," said the Queen.

"I've noticed, Captain, that you seem to sneeze quite a bit when the dogs are present, isn't that so?"

"I beg your pardon?" he said.

"Ma'am, do you think that Duchess would let me hold her?" said Lady Diggleton. "I should like to attempt an experiment."

Duchess looked nervous, but Penelope nodded to her. *It will be okay.*

Lady Diggleton picked up Duchess and held her as gently as could be. Then she held her close to Captain Clutterbeak's face.

"ACHOO! ACHOO! ACHOO!" he sneezed.

She moved Duchess away, and he stopped sneezing.

She moved Duchess back toward the captain, and he started sneezing even more intensely than before.

"All right!" the captain exclaimed. "Please! Get that dog away from me, and I shall tell you the truth!"

The Queen waved her hand as if to say *proceed*.

"It's true," he said. "I framed Duchess. Because I can't stand dogs! *I detest dogs!* I prefer birds! And—*achoo!*—I am *allergic* to dogs! But has anyone noticed? No, they have not! After years of loyal service, not a soul cared that I have been sniffling and sneezing every day since Her Majesty brought home that infernal creature! *Achoo!* So, when I entered your chambers, ma'am, and learned that the ring was gone, I spied Duchess's collar next to her bed. Suddenly I realized that this could be my chance to get rid of her once and for all! *Achoo!* I asked everyone to leave the room and gathered evidence to frame her. Then I came downstairs and made the most convincing case I could. And you believed it! *Achoo!* You all believed it!"

At this point it was quite obvious that

the captain was overwhelmed by his circumstances, and he threw himself on his knees. "But the ring was already gone when I stepped into your room. *Ah—ah—*I swear it upon my life! Oh, why didn't I destroy the evidence when I had the chance?" He picked up the gold brush and flung it across the room.

Everyone watched as it sailed over their heads and landed next to Penelope with a thud. It could have struck her, of course, but instead this was a most wonderful stroke of luck.

There's more than one scent on this brush, Penelope thought, bending down to sniff it.

A scent that I know.

A scent that could only belong to one creature . . . Dreadful Squirrel!

Chapter Twelve

Penelope tore out of the room, barking with all her might.

"Where are you going?" Duchess barked after her.

"To find the Canis Diamond! Follow me!" she cried.

Duchess raced after Penelope, the Queen raced after Duchess, Lady Diggleton raced after the Queen, Lady Picklebottom raced after Lady Diggleton, and the captain raced after them all. Mr. Weeby saw them running as he sat in the drawing room with a cup of tea, so he raced after them too!

Exiting the castle, Penelope darted to a spot under the window of the Queen's bedchambers. *Just as I hoped!* she thought. *There's a scent trail here for sure.*

She followed it across the great lawn, around the Round Tower, back toward the kitchen garden, until it ended at the raspberry patch. Penelope

peered through the leaves, her hackles
standing on end. In the shadows, she
could just make out two buckteeth and
a skinny tail. Surely you know who
she saw.

Penelope was
quick, but Dreadful
Squirrel was
quicker.

He dashed through the kitchen garden, over the pole beans, through the radishes, and past the potatoes.

Penelope *almost* had him clutched in her jaws, but suddenly Dreadful Squirrel leaped into a tree, where he jumped from one branch to another and disappeared into his nest amongst a canopy of leaves.

No! Penelope thought. *I can't let him get away this time!*

Duchess joined her and both dogs began to bark at the nest high above, while Dreadful Squirrel looked down with the trace of a smile on his gap-toothed face.

Lady Diggleton turned to the Queen. "I think there's something up there."

"I agree," said the Queen. "Ladies,

let us knock that nest down!"

The Queen, Lady Diggleton, and Lady Picklebottom began to push on the tree's trunk, rocking it back and forth with such ferocity that the nest came tumbling down and landed at their feet!

Dreadful Squirrel raced away as everyone gasped. The nest was filled with gold coins, a rather shocking number of raspberry tarts, and—the Canis Diamond ring!

"It's my ring!" the Queen said, reaching down to pick it up.

"I cannot believe it!" said Lady Diggleton.

"Nor can I!" shouted Lady Picklebottom.

The Queen turned to Duchess and Penelope. "Good dogs!" she said. "I am most impressed! Duchess, you are a very good dog indeed!"

Duchess was so happy she was positively glowing, as, for once, this was true.

Duchess and Penelope listened as Lady Diggleton, Lady Picklebottom, Mr. Weeby, and the Queen put the rest of the pieces together as they had tea. When she thought about it carefully, Lady Diggleton remembered that Mr. Tippletattle at the newspaper had warned her that there was a thief in their midst.

"But how did the squirrel get from Mayfair to Windsor Castle?" asked Lady Picklebottom.

Lady Diggleton thought a moment. "You know, he may have been a stowaway in my luggage. That squirrel seems to have a fascination with Penelope and is often around to torment her—and we both know how much he loves to steal raspberry tarts."

"Which is why my desserts went missing!" added the Queen. "Not to mention that Dreadful Squirrel must have crept into my room through the open window. It is far too high for any human to climb, but an animal can make easy work of it."

"But why would a squirrel—even a dreadful one—steal a ring?" said Lady Picklebottom.

"I believe I can be of some assistance here," said Mr. Weeby. "Few people in England can be called experts in animal behavior—and of course, I would be the last person to claim myself as such. Nevertheless, I do know quite a bit about many species, squirrels being one of them—"

"Oh, do get on with it," said the Queen, stroking Duchess, who was curled up comfortably in her lap.

"Of course, ma'am," said Mr. Weeby. "Squirrels are known to decorate their nests with all manner of pretty things. Flowers, seed pods, and things that sparkle, such as jewelry and gold coins."

"That is incredible," said Lady Diggleton.

"And to think, if Captain Clutterbeak hadn't tried to frame my lovely Duchess, he would not be on his way to the Confinement for Calamitous Captains," said the Queen.

"It is a shame," said Lady Diggleton.

"Not to me," said Lady Picklebottom. "I knew there was something wrong with that man from the very moment I laid eyes upon him. That sniffling nose. The way he frowned at the dogs. Only I—who once had such distaste for pups—would know that sort on the spot."

"So, what do you think, ma'am?" asked Lady Diggleton, reaching for a biscuit and giving it to Penelope. "Is the Canis Diamond really cursed?"

"Of course not!" the Queen said.

"Nevertheless, I do not think I shall wear it again for some time, just in case."

Everyone laughed as Duchess approached Penelope.

"I think I shall go for a walk," she said. "Would you like to join me?"

If Penelope was surprised by the invitation, she did not let it show. Instead, she said, "I should like that very much."

Outside, the weather was warm. Sunlight filtered through jewel-green trees while a small brook burbled nearby.

"May I ask you a question, Duchess?" Penelope said.

"You may," Duchess said.

"I do not wish to offend you, but when we first met, you were rather unkind."

"Unfortunately, that is true," said Duchess.

"But why? I should think being the Queen's prized pup would bring out one's gentler nature."

Duchess panted, and for a moment she remained in deep thought.

"It is not as easy to be the Royal Canine as you may think. From the moment I was chosen by the Queen, I was 'the special one.' My brothers and sisters no longer wished to play with me, and other puppies began to tease me for sport. I became different, and some dogs do not consider that to be a good thing."

"Do you think it was jealousy that

made other dogs behave so poorly?"

"Perhaps. Although, to be honest, I brought much of it upon myself. I became haughty and snobbish. I sulked and kept to myself. My behavior was embarrassing and rather horrendous to be honest, and I cannot tell you how sorry I am for the way I treated you."

"I accept your apology. But please do not be too hard on yourself," Penelope said.

"I must be. For I am a bad dog," Duchess said, looking away in shame.

Penelope looked at her. "Just because you did things that were bad does not mean that *you* are bad."

Duchess looked up and gave a small wag. "That is most kind, my friend—if I may call you a friend?"

"I shall insist that you do," Penelope said, "and I shall call you the same."

Duchess smiled as she tried to hide a yawn.

"Are you as tired as I?" asked Penelope, sensing her friend needed a nap.

"I am," Duchess admitted.

"That looks like a lovely place to rest, does it not?" Penelope said, nodding toward a nearby willow tree that was surrounded by daffodils that were just opening their petals for spring.

"I believe it does," said Duchess.

Nearby, Miss Greenstalk and Miss Berrycloth were grazing. They stopped to watch the dogs curl up together.

"I told youuu," said Miss Greenstalk,

"that one day Duchess would find a friend."

"Nooo, I'm the one who told youuu," said Miss Berrycloth.

"Youuu are quite wrong, dear friend."

"No, youuu are the wrong one."

The two cows grinned at each other, like the friends they were, as Penelope and Duchess drifted off to sleep to the soothing sound of the mooing, gossipy cows.

This is how the two dogs remained for the better part of the afternoon, while their friendship lasted for the rest of their days.

🐾

Now, you may find this a happy ending, and it was—for most.

Early in the evening, the dogs sat
in the garden and watched Lady
Diggleton and Lady Picklebottom
receive a medal from the Queen for
their work with the Ladies' Society

for the Relief of Lost Dogs. Mr. Weeby, of course, congratulated himself to anyone who would listen for training Duchess to accept a friend. All were quite content, in fact. Except for one.

High in a nearby tree, Dreadful
Squirrel watched. He chittered to
himself as he flicked his tail, thinking
about the mischief he would cause
when Penelope returned to Mayfair.
He had many ideas for how to get his
revenge, and would have plenty of time
to choose which way would be best.

Thinking of the possibilities,
Dreadful Squirrel grinned his dreadful
grin. His happy ending, he decided,
was yet to come.